DRAGON STORM

ELLIS AND PATHSEEKER

Alastair Chisholm

illustrated by Eric Deschamps

A STEPPING STONE BOOK™

Random House 🏠 New York

CONTENTS

This is a work of fiction. Names, characters, places, and incidents either are the product of the author's imagination or are used fictitiously. Any resemblance to actual persons, living or dead, events, or locales is entirely coincidental.

Text copyright © 2022 by Alastair Chisholm
Cover art and interior illustrations copyright © 2022 by Eric Deschamps

All rights reserved. Published in the United States by Random House Children's Books, a division of Penguin Random House LLC, New York. Originally published in paperback in slightly different form in the United Kingdom by Nosy Crow, Ltd, London, in 2022.

Random House and the colophon are registered trademarks and A Stepping Stone Book and the colophon are trademarks of Penguin Random House LLC.

Visit us on the Web!
rhcbooks.com

Educators and librarians, for a variety of teaching tools, visit us at
RHTeachersLibrarians.com

Library of Congress Cataloging-in-Publication Data is available upon request
ISBN 978-0-593-47960-5 (paperback) —
ISBN 978-0-593-47961-2 (library binding) — ISBN 978-0-593-47962-9 (ebook)

Printed in the United States of America
10 9 8 7 6 5 4 3 2 1
First American Edition

Random House Children's Books supports the
First Amendment and celebrates the right to read.

IN THE LAND OF DRACONIS, THERE ARE NO DRAGONS.

Once, there were. Once, humans
and dragons were friends and guarded
the land. They were wise, and strong, and
created the great city of Rivven together.

But then came the Dragon Storm, and the
dragons retreated from the world
of humans. To the men and women of
Draconis, they became legend and myth.

And so, these days, in the land of Draconis,
there are no dragons. . . .

Or so people thought.

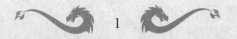

1
ELLIS

"The king! The king is coming. Hurry up!"

Cara and Tom dragged Ellis along the streets of Rivven, scrambling and squeezing through the crowd. Ellis clutched his notebook and tried to read as they ran.

"Which way?" shouted Tom.

"Left!" called Ellis. "Take a left here!" He turned, but the crowd swept him along and he lost his balance. Tom pulled him back with one

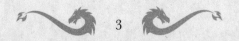

powerful hand. Together they forced a path through the crush and reached the bottom of a narrow lane.

"Are you sure?" asked Cara, peering up.

Ellis nodded. "This is Rat Lane. It cuts up to Hill Terrace. It's quite an interesting side street because—"

"Come on!" cried Tom. "They're nearly here!"

The three friends scrambled up the hill. Within a minute they reached the top of the lane, coming out onto a quiet corner of Hill Terrace. They skidded to a halt.

Tom grinned. "Perfect!"

At the heart of Rivven was a huge rocky hill that towered above the city. On top of the hill was the Royal Palace, with steep white walls

and flags flying in the breeze. A road curled down from the palace gates and opened out into a wide cobbled street that passed below Hill Terrace.

This was King Street, and today it was the route of the Spring Parade. The crowd heaved and pushed below them, but from their perch Ellis, Tom, and Cara had a perfect view. They watched the parade roll past.

First, there was the King's Guard. The horses were dressed in their finest saddles and wore polished buckles, and the riders' breastplates and swords gleamed in the pale sunshine. At their lead trotted Captain Hork, head of the King's Guard, puffing his chest out in glory and wearing his extra-tall head plume.

The royal household followed, all the top servants in their finest outfits—the men in red breeches and jackets, the women in long, flowing yellow dresses. They waved and smiled at the cheering spectators. Next there was a marching band, with drums, and brass horns, and long trumpets hung with flags. The musicians walked in perfect time as the rat-a-tat-tat of the drums echoed off the city buildings.

And then came the king.

His carriage shimmered with gold on every surface. Ornate curls and whirls decorated each side, and it was pulled by six horses with shiny black coats. The carriage was open-topped, carrying King Godfic, His Most Royal Majesty, Ruler of Rivven and the Land of Draconis, Defender of the Realm, and Dragon Scourge.

Ellis and the others watched from above as the carriage rolled past and the crowd cheered.

"Huh," said Tom. "I thought he'd be taller."

King Godfic sat hunched in a white fur robe. A golden crown rested on his head, and he appeared to be bored. He waved lazily to the crowd on either side, but didn't pay them much attention.

Behind him rolled another carriage. This one had only four horses. Its gold designs were almost as glorious. When the crowd saw the second carriage, they cheered again.

"It's the prince and princess!" shouted Tom.

Prince Harald, blond-haired and handsome, grinned at the crowd. His tunic was scarlet, with shining silver thread. He waved as if delighted, pointing to the homemade banners and occasionally turning to make comments to his younger sister, the princess.

Princess Skye did not respond. She wore a beautiful blue gown the color of the summer

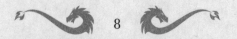

sky, but she kept her arms folded, making the dress look wrinkled. She gazed out at the

crowd, her mouth turned down and a sour expression on her face.

"She looks like fun," said Cara, and Tom snorted. He turned to Ellis.

"Hey, what are you doing?" he asked. "You're missing the best parts!"

"Hmm?" Ellis looked up from his notes. "I was just thinking, when we came up Rat Lane we could have turned onto Candle Street and avoided the crowd, see? It would have been quicker."

Cara laughed. "Ellis, we're *here* now. You found us the best place to view the parade— come and watch!"

The royal carriages passed. Then came the princess's ladies-in-waiting, followed by friends

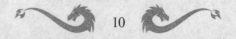

of Prince Harald. After that, there were royal courtiers, more horsemen, another band, marching troops . . . and then the procession was gone.

The crowd dispersed, and Ellis and the others headed back through town.

"Where does the parade go now?" asked Cara.

"Around to the Plaza," muttered Ellis, without looking up. "Over Lion Bridge, through Queen Lira's Gardens, around Merrin Wall, and back to the palace." He jotted something down.

"You spend all your time scribbling," said Tom. "You never *see* anything. That was the Spring Parade!"

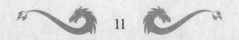

Ellis frowned. "I saw it. Parade, king, prince, princess. Look, I made notes." He held up his notebook.

Cara said, "Ellis doesn't care about the parade, Tomás. He only cares about what comes *after*."

"What's that?" asked Tom.

"The Maze Festival," said Ellis shyly, and Tom laughed.

"Oh, of course!"

At the end of the Spring Celebrations came the Maze Festival. Every year, the citizens of Rivven were allowed into the palace grounds for one day. There was food and drink and entertainment. Most exciting to Ellis was the competition to solve three ornate mazes in the palace gardens. The competition was meant for children, but the mazes were hard enough to challenge even grown-ups.

"Ellis has been thinking about it for weeks," laughed Cara. "I bet he's got a brand-new notebook all ready!"

They reached a small, broken-down cottage tucked into a shadowed alleyway. Cara glanced around and opened the ancient door. The others followed her through the doorway. Once inside, Tom opened another, smaller door, which led to a corridor far too long for the tiny cottage, a corridor that twisted in strange ways and moved under their feet as they walked.

"I think I'll have a go at these mazes too,"

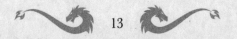

said Cara. "Give you a bit of competition, eh?"

Ellis grinned. "All right. If you like coming in second place."

"Ooh!" said Cara. "A challenge, is it, Ellis? You're on!"

They laughed as they reached the final doorway. And then the three ordinary children, happy after a morning of seeing the king on parade, passed through the doorway. . . .

And into the Dragonseer Guild Hall.

2
DRAGONSEER

The Guild Hall was a vast cavern, so large it was hard to see the far end. Ellis had spent months mapping it out. From the maze of tunnels and chambers at the north end to the ruined towers to the west, Ellis had explored more than anyone, and there were still parts he knew nothing about. The Guild Hall held the huts, training ground, and dormitories that made up the Dragonseer Guild. As they entered, the children sighed. It was good to be back.

The air shimmered beside them, and a dragon appeared.

She was long-tailed, sharp-toothed, and small for a dragon but fierce-looking. She seemed to match the color of the hall behind her, like camouflage, but with a silver edge. The dragon rushed toward Cara. Cara hugged the creature's neck.

"Hey, Silverthief," she said, scratching the dragon's ears. "How's it going?"

Beside her, Tom summoned his dragon, Ironskin. She was huge, and her dark-red skin crackled with lines of orange-yellow, like fire.

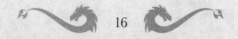

But her expression was kind. Like Tom, she was never hurtful.

Ellis smiled, closed his eyes, reached out beyond the world of humans, and waited for his dragon: Pathseeker.

The Dragonseer Guild was a secret place, hidden from normal people, including King Godfic and his soldiers. The Guild was a place for people with a special power, who could see things others couldn't. These talented few could see beyond the human world, to somewhere very different. . . .

A place of *dragons*.

Chancellor Berin liked to tell them how grand the Guild used to be. "Once, there were thousands of dragons in our world. The skies were full of them! And beside each one was a *dragonseer*. And just as every dragonseer is unique, so was every dragon. They were *our* dragons. And we were their humans."

The bond between dragonseer and dragon was a link between worlds—a doorway that a dragon could step through. Ellis felt a flicker in his mind, and smiled. When he opened his eyes, Pathseeker was there.

Pathseeker wasn't the biggest of dragons, or the smallest. She was a few feet taller than Ellis, with a thick neck, four short legs, a strong tail, and a sturdy, round body. Her skin was a mixture of greens, like the leaves of a tree on a windy day.

"Hey, Path," Ellis murmured.

"Hello, Ellis." Pathseeker's voice was deep and calm, like a river. She leaned her head down toward him, and they rubbed noses.

A bell sounded, and the children hurried to their classes, their dragons alongside them.

This afternoon they were in Drun's class.

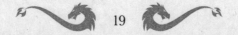

Drun taught dragon care and summoning. He had his own hut inside the Guild Hall. It was a large, round building with a chimney up the middle. Like all the children, Ellis had once sat inside that hut, with Drun and Chancellor Berin, learning how to summon. He remembered peering into the fire, listening to Drun's voice. And then feeling that magical connection as the dragon Pathseeker had come into the human world.

But today Drun was sitting outside, in his old brown leather clothes, scratching his beard and smiling. Ellis and the others sat around him in a half-circle with their dragons.

There was Mira, small but quick, often

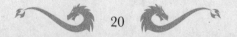

covered in grease from machinery. Her dragon was Flameteller, a creature whose angular shape and brown and bronze colors made him look almost like a machine himself. Then Connor, tall and pale, kind of a know-it-all, and his dragon, Lightspirit. She had a long, thin body with short legs. Beside them was easygoing Kai, who got along with everyone. His dragon, Boneshadow, was white, with a striking red cross on her chest. And finally there was Erin, the tallest and strongest of the group. Beside her sat an enormous and fierce dragon called Rockhammer.

"Afternoon, all," said Drun cheerfully, once they had settled. "Lovely day, isn't it?"

The children laughed. Inside the Guild

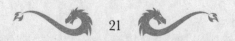

Hall, every day was the same—the globes above them glowed like tiny suns, and there were no clouds or rain.

"Today I'm going to talk about your dragon's *power*," said Drun. "Each dragon has its own special power, and it comes when they most need it." He smiled. "Some o' you have already found yours, right?"

The dragons Ironskin and Silverthief preened a little. Ironskin could create a magic shield around herself and others—a power she'd discovered when she and Tom had rescued Tom's parents from a fire. And Silverthief, Cara's dragon, could actually turn invisible for a short while.

Drun smiled and nodded to the others. "You'll all get yours in time."

"What will it be?" asked Erin.

Connor scoffed. "Nobody knows until it *happens*," he said. "Don't you know that?"

Erin bristled, but Drun held up a hand. "It's true," he said gently. "But we get some clues. You know the world of dragons is a world of . . . ideas, I suppose. They get their shapes in our world when they first connect to their humans. In some ways, they're like you. . . ."

Ellis looked at Pathseeker. She was average-sized for a dragon, but strong, and Ellis was the same—not tall, but sturdy, with strong legs for hiking. Ellis's skin was deep brown, while Pathseeker's was leafy green. But there was something else.

It had been almost a year since Ellis had met Pathseeker. He'd been camping in the woods north of Rivven. He was sitting by his campfire and writing out maps when he heard a whispering voice say, "That second pathway went left, you know, not right."

Ellis had spun around but seen nothing behind him. When he'd turned back, there were a pair of eyes, gazing at him from the fire!

Ellis knew he should have been terrified. But there had been something in those eyes he'd recognized—a faraway, restless look,

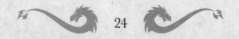

always wanting to see where the next path went.

When he'd returned to the city the next day, he was convinced he'd had a most peculiar dream. Then he found the king's clerk Malik waiting for him, and was offered an apprenticeship. But not as a clerk—as a dragonseer. His life had changed forever that day.

Back in class, Drun continued talking. "Their power will be somethin' you need," he said. "It will be somethin' to do with *you*." He looked at each of the children in turn. "Have a think what it might be."

That evening, Ellis and Pathseeker
sat curled up outside Ellis's
dorm. They worked on
maps. The sound of
laughter drifted from
inside the dining
hut behind them.
Ellis ignored it.

"I hope your
power is to be
able to find
a route to
anywhere," he said. "Then we'd be able to
map *everywhere*."

The dragon's eyes crinkled. "Maybe," she

said, nodding. She stretched. "How was the parade?"

"I went up Rat Lane," said Ellis.

"Hmm," mused Pathseeker. "If you'd gone up Candle Street, you would have avoided some of the crowd."

"I *know*!" laughed Ellis. "I realized later."

"But how was the parade itself?" asked Pathseeker.

"Tom and Cara enjoyed it," said Ellis. "It's weird . . . King Godfic hates the idea of dragons—he'd probably think we were his enemy!" He sighed. "Chancellor Berin says he's just misguided, and we have to be patient."

"What about you?" asked Pathseeker. "Did you like it?"

Ellis shrugged. "It was fine. I wasn't really paying attention."

The dragon's chest rumbled against his back as she chuckled. Ellis and Pathseeker saw things the same way. She loved helping him map out the world, and neither of them was very interested in anything else.

Ellis yawned and closed his notebook. "Enough for today. Busy day tomorrow."

"Oh?" asked Pathseeker. "What are we up to?"

Ellis's eyes gleamed. "We're going to find the true location of the Guild Hall."

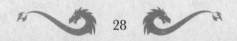

3
LOOK UP

The next day, Ellis was back on Hill Terrace with his notebook, scowling at the city.

The location of the Dragonseer Guild Hall nagged at him all the time. No one in the Guild would tell the children where it was. They knew how to reach the little door that led inside, but after that there was a maze of passages and corridors to go through before reaching the Hall. Ellis had a good sense of

direction, but the maze confused him. The passages *moved*, turning in different ways every time he walked along them.

The Hall could be anywhere in the kingdom—but where? Rivven was the capital of Draconis. The huge Palace Rock sat in the center, and a lot of the city was built over older buildings and cellars. And one thing was clear: there was nowhere big enough to hold the enormous Guild Hall.

It had to be underground, he thought. But there were old rivers, tunnels, sewers, and crypts below the city to consider. Ellis had studied the old maps. He couldn't find a space anywhere that made sense.

"Hey, Ellis!"

Ellis turned. It was Tom, carrying a heavy sack. Tom's dad was a blacksmith, and these days he secretly helped the Guild by making training harnesses for dragons. Every now and then Tom went home and returned with a bag of new equipment.

"What are you doing?" Tom asked.

Ellis sighed. "Trying to find the Guild Hall, again."

Tom nodded. "You'll get there. Nice morning, isn't it?"

Ellis looked around. The sun was low but warm, and the early-morning mist was burning off. He shrugged. "Sure."

Tom grinned. "Ellis, you should try experiencing things a bit more, you know? Look up now and then!"

Ellis frowned. "I look up." He showed Tom his latest map notes. "See, that's St. Bellan's Church spire there, and that's the palace, and that's the tannery chimney. They're really tall, so they make good landmarks, and then you can triangulate your location and get really accurate—"

"That's not what I meant," said Tom gently.

He rummaged in his bag and pulled out a strip of cloth. "Close your eyes."

Puzzled, Ellis did so, and Tom fastened the cloth over his eyes.

"What are you doing?"

"Trust me. Now, where are you?"

"At the corner of Hill Terrace."

"Okay. Now . . ." Tom lifted Ellis up, turned around, and put him down again. Ellis couldn't tell which way he was facing anymore. Then Tom said, "Follow me."

"This is silly."

"Trust me!" Tom took Ellis's hands and guided him. Downhill a little, then left, left again, right.

"Okay," said Tom at last. "Where are you now?"

Ellis frowned. "How would I know?"

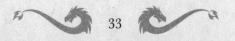

Tom laughed. "Well, try this: what can you *smell*?"

Ellis sniffed. There was fresh morning air, fish, a tang of salt? And stewing meat . . .

"And what can you feel? What are the stones like?"

The cobbles under his boots were round and worn smooth. Ellis shifted a foot and felt the edges. Old?

"Well . . . ," Ellis said.

"Is it warm? Cold?" Tom asked.

It was warm. But when Ellis turned, it became cooler. The sun had been on his face. It was morning, so the sun would be in the east.

"I'm facing east," he said. "And I can smell fish. I'm near the harbor. And . . . I can hear people chatting— we're near an inn. And the cobbles are smooth. . . ." He nodded. "I'm on the Causeway, leading down to the harbor, outside the Hungry Dog tavern."

Tom pulled the blindfold off, and Ellis saw his grinning face. "Well done!"

Ellis shrugged. "But what was the point?"

"Just . . . try *experiencing* things now and

then," said Tom. "Look up, see what's really there—don't just write it all down. You might find more than you expect."

"Um . . . okay," said Ellis. He didn't really see what Tom was getting at, but he nodded.

Tom smiled. "See you later!" He headed off toward the Guild Hall entrance, waving.

Ellis watched him go. Then he made a note about the cobbles and carried on searching.

4

THE MAZE
FESTIVAL

A few days later, it was the Maze Festival.

It was a beautiful spring day. The people in the crowd were in a good mood, laughing and joking and jostling past each other. The end of the Spring Celebrations was always fun. It was the one day when the palace grounds were opened to commoners.

Queen Matilda had started the tradition a

few years ago. Ellis remembered seeing her standing on top of one of the walls, waving and welcoming everyone in. Inside, there were tables of food, barrels of ale, musicians, jugglers, and jesters. There were even firemasters, who could make explosions of colored smoke. It was a day of magic.

Queen Matilda was no longer at the palace. They said she'd had a furious disagreement with the king and left. No one knew where she'd gone. But the celebrations continued, and everyone was looking forward to a good day. Ellis couldn't wait to see the mazes.

Chancellor Berin had given them permission to go. "Remember," she'd warned

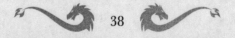

them, looking serious, "you will be in the Royal Palace grounds—you must let *no one* see your powers, do you understand?" The children had all nodded, and she'd chuckled. "And have fun!"

"I don't get it, Ellis," said Mira as they approached the gates. "You said you did the mazes before. Don't you know how to solve them already?"

"They change them every year," said Connor, always pleased to know something others didn't. "They replant the hedges and rebuild everything. Even the Dark Maze. They bind the branches to make different paths. It's a closely guarded secret. The Maze Guardians only know parts of the whole thing."

Mira frowned. "Maze Guardians? That sounds mysterious."

"They're really the head gardeners," said Ellis. He smiled. "But it's true. After the festival, everyone will know how to find their way through all the mazes. But right now, *nobody* does."

The palace grounds were huge, hidden within the palace walls. There were lawns, small groves of trees, a pond with a bridge across it, gentle hills, and flower beds. Spaced between them were the three mazes that had been part of the grounds for centuries: the Green Maze, the Silver Maze, and the Dark Maze. Occasionally people wandered over to the mazes, trying to peek in, but lines of stern-looking gardeners blocked the entrances.

At ten o'clock a fanfare of trumpets sounded. The palace gates opened, and out came a procession of guards, courtiers, and

then King Godfic's carriage, carrying the king and Prince Harald. The crowd roared in approval! The carriage stopped at a stage, and King Godfic stepped onto it and sat on a tall golden throne. Prince Harald sat on one of two smaller thrones, slightly farther back. Ellis peered around, but he couldn't see the princess.

A jolly man, wearing the traditional collared vest of the Master Gardener, stepped up onto the stage. He bowed to King Godfic and Prince Harald. Then the Master Gardener turned to the audience and lifted his hands.

"Good people of Draconis!" he called in a hearty voice. "His Majesty King Godfic welcomes you to the last day of the Spring Celebrations: the Maze Festival!"

The crowd cheered. King Godfic, perched on his throne and talking with an advisor, turned and waved halfheartedly.

The Master Gardener continued. "If any children would like to take part and be the first to attempt to solve the Three Mazes, then come forward now and take your flag!"

Ellis, Cara, and Connor came forward, as well as a few local children. They approached a table in front of the stage. The table was covered in flags of different colors, each one on a long stick. A smiling woman in green took each child's name and gave them a flag.

"Now," she said, "the maze walls are quite

tall, but if you get lost, just wave this as high as you can, and we'll come and find you, all right?"

Ellis took his flag, the same shade of green as Pathseeker. "I won't need it," he said.

The woman laughed. "I wouldn't be too sure," she said. "We've had some fun designing this year's mazes!"

When they had their flags, the children lined up in front of the first challenge: the Green Maze.

The Green Maze was made of tall box hedges cut into beautiful neat walls. It had three entrances, and the contestants lined up around them. There were about thirty children, grinning and laughing, some fooling

around. Ellis checked his backpack again, pulled out his new notebook and a pencil stub, then held his breath.

"The Green Maze!" called the speaker. "Brave adventurers, enter if you dare! Find your way to the very center, collect the ribbon

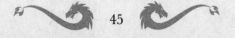

that matches your flag, and escape the maze.
First contestant out with their ribbon is the
winner! Are you ready?"

Ellis glanced at Cara and Connor, and they
grinned back.

"Steady?"

Ellis leaned forward over the starting
line.

"Go!"

5
THE
GREEN MAZE

Ellis and the others raced toward the entrances as the crowd cheered behind them. Ellis headed for the corner entrance, with Cara picking the left and Connor the right. The walls of this maze were straight, and there were many openings on either side of the path. Ellis counted them as he walked. Children rushed past him, and he glimpsed some of the others through the hedges, but Ellis took his time. He carefully marked the routes he took. When he was sure he was alone, he stopped and concentrated. After a moment he felt a shimmer and the familiar connection in his heart. . . .

"Path?" he whispered.

Hello! came Pathseeker's voice in his mind. Ellis grinned. It was too dangerous to bring the dragon all the way into the human world—he imagined how some of the other children would react if they ran through the maze and saw her!—but he loved talking with her.

How are you getting on?

"Just started," he murmured. He looked up at the green walls of thick hedge, tall and solid. The sounds of the other children faded slightly as he walked.

He wandered along, keeping one hand brushing against the left wall, and whenever it opened up, he turned left and made another note on his map. This was a good way to get a feel for the maze. If he did it for long enough, it might even take him to the center. After a while he felt he could see the outline of the maze in his mind.

"Ready?" he murmured.

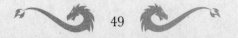

Oh, yes. He could almost feel Pathseeker nod.
At the next turn, he made a right, toward the
center. He recorded his route, each junction
and entrance, but he could already tell that
this maze was simple. He knew where he was.
The overall pattern was a spiral. He worked
his way through the layers, occasionally back-
tracking, but always closing in on the center of
the maze.

Ellis passed some of the other children in
the middle layers. They were laughing and
chasing each other. He smiled at them, but
continued with his own route.

I think we're getting close! whispered Pathseeker,
and Ellis nodded. He followed the hedge
around one last bend.

He was there.

Yes!

Ellis grinned. The center of the maze was an open circle, with a table covered in ribbons of every color. With delight, he saw that none of the ribbons had been taken yet. They were first!

He found his green ribbon and turned to leave. All he had to do now was find his way back. He had his map for that, but the route was clear in his mind—left, left, right, second left, long corridor, follow the curve, left . . .

And then the maze *rippled*.

Ellis staggered and almost fell. What was that?

Ellis!

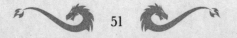

He spun, and put out a hand to steady himself. The hedge wall of the maze was firm and neat, prickly under his fingers. Looking up, he stared down a long corridor, and for a moment he saw the strangest thing— a reflection of himself, staring back!

Ellis gasped. The reflection's mouth was an O of astonishment. They gazed at each other. But there was something wrong. The maze behind his reflection wasn't green. There were no hedges at all. Instead the maze was dark and shadowy, like twisted roots from an ancient tree.

The maze rippled again, and this time he *did* fall. When Ellis got back to his feet, the reflection was gone. The hedge was a hedge again, the maze back to normal.

Ellis blinked.

"Um . . . ," he said.

Ellis, what was that? gasped Pathseeker's voice in his mind. Ellis shook his head.

"You saw it too?"

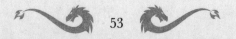

Yes!

He looked around. Everything seemed normal. The hedge was solid and thick. The path was gravel again, and he was the only one on it. There were no reflections.

Ellis shook his head again and glanced at the map.

"Come on," he muttered. "Let's get out."

He followed the route, slowly at first but faster as his confidence came back. Now he could hear the roar of the crowd outside, he could see one of the entrances, and he burst out, holding his ribbon up!

He stopped.

The crowd was already cheering. In front of

him there was a figure holding a gray ribbon high in the air.

"Oh," said Ellis, crestfallen.

He vaguely remembered her from the start—a girl in shabby gray clothes and a shapeless hood that hid her face. Even now, she kept her head down.

The crowd cheered and roared. The girl walked to the table and handed over her ribbon.

How did she do it? asked

Pathseeker. *I don't understand—we made it to the center of the maze first!*

Ellis shook his head and sighed. He trotted across to the table and handed his own ribbon over. The lady sitting at the table smiled.

"Well done," she said warmly. "Second place for you!"

Ellis nodded. He turned to the girl, but she was already walking away. He moved to the side and waited for the others to arrive.

Cara was next, emerging ten minutes after Ellis and blinking at the crowd. Ellis knew she didn't like being the center of attention. Cara slunk over to the table and thrust her ribbon across. Then another child emerged from the maze, someone Ellis didn't know, and then Connor. Connor glowered when he saw Ellis and Cara already there, then grinned and threw up his hands.

"Got lost coming out," he called. "Next time!"

Ellis grinned back. More children came out, and the judges waited a few minutes longer before one of them blew a long whistle. Inside the maze, anyone still lost had to hold up their flag and wave it high, so the Maze Guardians could find them.

"Well done, all!" called the Master Gardener. "And congratulations to everyone who managed to solve the Green Maze.

"Next up: the Silver Maze. Who dares enter its silvery depths?"

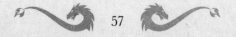

Ellis, Cara, and Connor shared glances. "Ready?" asked Cara.

Ellis wondered if he should say something about what he'd seen. But nobody else seemed alarmed. Had he imagined it? He shook his head, checked his bag, and looked across at the girl in gray. Her hood was still over her head. Her fists were clenching and unclenching.

"Ready," he said.

This time, said Pathseeker.

6
THE
SILVER MAZE

The crowd moved around the palace, toward the Winter Groves.

The Winter Groves looked as if they were covered in ice or snow. Everything was pale and white. Each plant had silvery-white leaves or long white stalks. The trees were silver birch or ash, shimmering in the faint breeze. Even the grass was white-tipped, as if on a frosty morning.

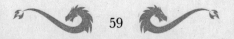

In the center stood the Silver Maze.

Its walls were metal, polished into mirrors and covered in patterns of silver leaves and vines. It looked like a fairy-tale castle in a magical frozen forest.

There was another royal platform. As Ellis watched, King Godfic and Prince Harald stepped out of their carriage and took their places. The Master Gardener stepped up again.

"Well, then!" he bellowed. "Who dares enter the Silver Maze? This torment of souls, this mechanical monstrosity?" He made a gruesome face, and the crowd laughed.

Ellis, Cara, and Connor stepped forward.

So did the girl in gray and some others—though fewer than before. Ellis watched the girl, but she didn't turn, or even look up. She had pulled a gold necklace from beneath her cloak and was clutching its pendant.

The Master Gardener lifted his flag and waited for silence.

"Ready?" he called. "Steady . . . GO!"

The girl in gray set off. Because she had won the first round, she got a thirty-second head start. She jogged toward the only entrance. Ellis watched in agony as the woman at the table carefully measured the time with an hourglass. When she brought her hand down, he raced into the maze.

The inside of the walls matched the outside: shimmering metal, polished so bright it reflected Ellis's face back to him as he ran. The floor was smooth black stone. Everything was so bright that it was easy to miss an entrance or a turn. Ellis moved more swiftly this time but stayed methodical. Whipping out his notebook, he made quick marks as he turned left and right. He wondered if he would see the girl, but she seemed to have picked a different path. He knew he didn't have long.

So this is the Silver Maze? asked Pathseeker. Ellis nodded.

"I did it last year," he muttered.

It's very bright. Is that what makes it difficult? All those mirrors are confusing.

"Partly," said Ellis. He took a left and then a quick right, marking as he ran. He began to hear a ticking sound, so he sped up. He wanted to get as far as he could before—

There was a click, and a wall slid up in front of him. Then he felt the floor move, and turn, and click again into place. The wall in front

of him slid back down. Now the path was different.

The maze changes! said Pathseeker's voice. She sounded excited, and Ellis grinned.

"I *know*," he said. "Isn't it great? It's in sections, and each section turns. It's *really* hard to map."

He studied his notes. You couldn't draw this maze, not when each part could suddenly turn. Instead he had raced through to try to get a single section clear in his head. The maze had turned *clockwise*. They had been facing north, and the center had been east.

"Straight ahead," he muttered.

Agreed.

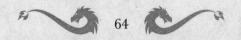

Ellis raced along, trying to get as far as possible before the next turn. He scribbled notes as he went.

"We're doing well!" he shouted. "We're nearly there. I can feel it!"

Pathseeker laughed. When they were map-making, she always felt very close. Now he could almost imagine her running beside him, her thick green skin rippling, her mouth open in delight at another turning, another junction, until—

"Oh!"

Ellis raced around a corner and skidded to a halt. The girl in gray was right ahead of him!

She was standing in the center of the maze,

next to the table of ribbons. She faced away from him. She was holding something and staring at it.

At first, Ellis was alarmed. He'd been talking to Pathseeker out loud—had the girl heard him? But she seemed completely engrossed, staring at the pendant that hung from her neck. Then she looked up, away from him, and gasped. Ellis looked up too.

The maze unfolded. The silver walls fell away. The black floors changed. This wasn't like the mechanical turning Ellis had felt before. This was like something melting, or becoming ghostly. The walls faded away into nothing. The effect spread, so that the world ahead seemed completely flat. But it went on for much too far. The maze couldn't possibly be that big. And then new walls rose up!

Ellis, what's happening?

Some of the walls were silver, some green. Some were brown and twisted, like old tree roots, moving and growing into shapes. Ellis felt the ground trembling. He could hear the green walls shooting up and tree roots sliding over each other.

"No, no, *no*," muttered the girl suddenly. She slumped against the table. "Stop *doing* this!"

"What's going on?" gasped Ellis.

The girl spun in shock and let go of the pendant. The maze snapped back into place. The roots and hedges disappeared, and the silver walls flickered back into existence.

"What's happening?" said Ellis. "What are you doing? What *is* that?"

He pointed to the pendant hanging from her necklace. It was a strange thing—large and heavy. It was gold and had eight sides. In the center was what looked like a diamond, but there seemed to be something inside. For

a strange moment, Ellis thought it looked like an eye.

"Get away!" shouted the girl. "Don't come near me!"

"But what's going *on*?" he tried. "Are you doing this?"

She ignored him, grabbed her ribbon, and ran off down the far corridor. Ellis started to run after her, then cursed. He ran back to the table, found his own ribbon, then went after the girl. But the ticking noise sounded again. Before he could leave the center, the silver walls around him slid up, and they turned.

"Pathseeker, what *was* that?" he demanded. "Was it magic?"

I'm not sure, said Pathseeker. *Perhaps . . . I've seen it before, I think. . . .*

The floor stopped moving, and the silver walls slid down again. Ellis tried to chase after the girl, but she could be anywhere now. He wasn't even going in the same direction as her.

Stop! hissed Pathseeker. *Ellis, you'll get lost.*

Ellis skidded to a halt. Pathseeker was right—this wasn't the way they had come in. He had to work out how to escape. But what was going on? Whatever the girl was doing, it had seemed to *change* the maze. Parts of it had looked like the hedges from the first maze. Other parts, he thought, were from the third maze, which they hadn't even reached yet!

And there was something about that pendant. The strange eight-sided setting with the diamond and something inside it.

Ellis turned, and turned again. Then he stopped. He realized that he wasn't paying attention. He carefully drew the corridors and junctions he'd passed, until he had a clear idea where he was. Then he set off again. The sound of the crowd outside got louder and louder as he got closer to the exit. Then, *finally,* he found the opening and left the maze.

The crowd cheered, but he could tell he wasn't first. Sure enough, there was the girl, standing to one side. She'd pulled her hood far down over her face. He could only make out shadows and a grim mouth. The pendant was tucked away again.

"Took your time," said a voice, and Ellis turned to see Cara grinning.

"You beat me?" he asked.

Cara grinned even wider. "Oh, I know a trick or two myself. What happened? I thought you were ahead of me."

Ellis frowned. "Did you—" He stopped, then tried again. "Did you see anything strange? In the maze?"

Cara looked puzzled. "Strange? Like what? You mean like the way it moves around?"

"No, I mean . . ." He shook his head. "I saw the girl, the one who keeps winning.

But she was doing something with a pendant on a necklace. And the maze kind of . . . *changed*."

Cara studied him. "Are you all right, Ellis? You didn't bump your head or something in there, did you?"

Ellis sighed. The two friends walked toward the table. "No. I can't explain it. It was like . . . I don't know. Just something about the pendant. It was eight-sided—like the one we saw down in the tunnels under the Guild Hall, remember?" Cara nodded. "And it looked like there was something *inside* it."

Beside him, Cara stopped walking and stiffened.

"It sounds weird," said Ellis, "but it almost looked like—"

"An eye," said Cara flatly.

Ellis blinked. "Yes! How did you know?"

Cara's face was serious. "I've seen it before," she said. "I know what it is. And it's very, *very* bad."

7
DRAGON'S EYE

"It's called a Dragon's Eye," said Cara. "It's incredibly dangerous."

The dragonseers were in the Arboretum, a small grove of trees near the Silver Maze. After the remaining children had made it out of the Silver Maze (or hoisted their flags to be rescued), the jolly Master Gardener had announced a break for lunch. Large wooden tables were brought out and piled high with

picnic food for the crowd. Ellis, Cara, and
Connor had grabbed a few things to eat and
now sat under an apple tree.

"How do you know?" asked Ellis. "Have you
seen one before?"

"I was . . ." Cara looked embarrassed. "I was somewhere I shouldn't have been. It was before I was a dragonseer." Nobody said anything. Everyone knew that before joining the Guild, Cara had scraped by on the streets of Rivven, sometimes even stealing to survive.

"Anyway, I saw one. It belonged to the king."

"What, King *Godfic*?" gasped Connor.

Cara nodded.

"So what *is* it?" asked Ellis.

Cara frowned. "I'm not sure," she admitted. "I told Chancellor Berin about it, but she didn't say much. Only that King Godfic shouldn't have a pendant like that. But I found information in some of the books at the Guild

Hall. It's a special kind of dragon magic. Not *good* dragon magic. The other kind."

Connor pulled out a notebook and flicked back through the pages. "Is this it?" he asked. He showed them a rough drawing of an eight-sided pendant that held a diamond. At the heart of the diamond was a fierce and angry eye. Ellis studied the picture and nodded.

"I heard Berin and Vice Chancellor Creedy talking about it," Connor said. "They seemed worried, so I read up on it. The pendant has *finding* magic. Like, if you wanted to find someone who was hiding, you could use this to find them."

"How?" Cara asked.

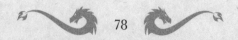

Connor shrugged. "The books didn't say. They were more about how you shouldn't use that type of magic and how something terrible happens to anyone who does."

He sat back, looking pleased with himself. Then his brow creased. "Oh, but *she's* using it!"

"I think she is," said Ellis. "I think she's trying to use it to solve the mazes. To . . . cheat."

He found it difficult to say. A maze was a puzzle, and solving the maze was the whole *point* of it. Why would you cheat? Why would you get something to tell you the answer? Why even *do* the puzzle? It made no sense to him.

"Do you think it's the same one the king

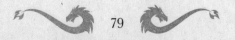

had?" asked Cara. "How can she have it? Who *is* she, anyway?"

Connor frowned. "If anyone could actually use it, they might be able to find the Dragonseer Guild Hall."

"So what do we do?"

"We could tell the Master Gardener," said Connor.

"Tell him what?" scoffed Cara. "That one of the competitors has an incredibly powerful ancient evil magic jewel, and they're using it to win a kids' Maze Festival cup?"

"Well, perhaps not," admitted Connor. "But what can we do?"

"Maybe we could catch the girl using it?

Take it off her then?" Cara looked at Ellis. "We could give it to Berin—she'd know what to do. Maybe we can all try to follow her?"

Ellis nodded. "Yes. We have to stop her. You can't cheat at mazes. It's not right."

"Agreed," said Connor. "Also, we have to stop her from using dark, evil magic."

Ellis shrugged. "Sure, that too."

The Master Gardener called to the crowd again, and the children headed to the third maze. This was meant to be the hardest of the three mazes. It was also the oldest. It was hundreds of years older than the others. Some people said it was older than the palace. *Some* people said it was older even than Rivven.

It was the Dark Maze.

Like the Green Maze, it was made from greenery. But instead of hedges forming neat, trim walls, there were huge and ancient trees— powerful oaks, twisted yews, beech trees with long gnarled branches and clawing twigs. This maze was different from the others. There were no straight lines here; it grew its own way, and every year it was different.

"The *Dark Maze*," uttered the Master Gardener, and the crowd went *ooooh*, and then laughed. The gardener grinned.

"Well, now. Who is brave enough to

challenge this *labyrinth of terror*?" he called.
Ellis looked across at the girl. She stepped
forward, her hood still pulled down over her
face. So did Ellis and Cara and Connor, along

with a few of the others who had finished the previous mazes.

This time the lady at the table gave Ellis a ball of green twine.

"We won't be able to see a flag," she said, smiling. "So you fasten the end to an entrance hook and unravel it as you go through, all right? If you get lost, you can just follow the string back."

Ellis nodded and walked toward the entrance to the maze. The girl ignored him. Cara and Connor joined Ellis.

"Remember," murmured Cara. "We follow the girl, and get the pendant before she has a chance to use it."

Ellis nodded.

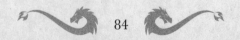

"Oh, there was something else!" said Connor, snapping his fingers. "I've just remembered. About the Dragon's Eye."

"What?" asked Cara.

"You can only use it if you're a dragonseer," said Connor. "Someone like us."

"Wait, what?" asked Cara. "Are you saying that girl's a *dragonseer*? But that's—"

"Ready!" shouted the Master Gardener. The crowd cheered, and Cara's words were lost.

"Steady! . . . Go!"

8
THE
DARK MAZE

The mystery girl started first again, and sprinted toward the dark entrance. She fastened the end of her gray ball of twine around one of the hooks and disappeared into the maze.

After thirty seconds Ellis fastened his own green string, and chased after her.

The Dark Maze was *very* dark. A few yards

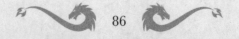

in, the lowest branches on each side of the path stretched up higher than Ellis could reach. The sky became a narrow blue strip above him. Sometimes even that disappeared as the branches joined together overhead. The light had to travel through twigs and leaves, and took on a murky, muddy color. Old roots grew out of the earth and tripped Ellis as he ran.

He kept his notebook open. Ellis and Pathseeker tried to track the direction of the paths as they twisted, while following the girl's gray string.

The maze wound onward. The roots of the trees were so thick they covered the ground, and Ellis had to clamber over them. Branches steered him into strange curving paths. The light grew dimmer. He kept his ball of twine firmly in his hands and pushed on toward the center, following the girl.

Ellis reached a little glade, where the trees opened up and let the sunshine in. An unusual-looking old lime tree was growing on one side. It was covered in beautiful white flowers that shone in the unexpected sunlight and gave

off a soft scent. Ellis took notes and looked for exits.

Ellis, whispered Pathseeker. *Something's wrong.*

Ellis stopped. "What's up?"

I don't know. The dragon's voice sounded nervous and unsure. *But there's something—*

The maze changed.

The roots under Ellis's feet faded and disappeared. He tripped over, sprawling flat on a neat gravel path.

"Ow!" He stared at his hands, grazed against the gravel. Where were the roots? This was more like the first maze! He turned and stared. The gnarled branches around him were gone. Smooth, neat green hedges had formed up around him instead.

"Path, it's happening again!" he shouted.

The girl must be doing something! said Pathseeker. *We have to catch her, Ellis!*

Ellis scrambled to his feet, found the gray twine, and staggered after it. The walls of the maze shifted as he ran. Now they seemed silver, glinting in sunlight. Then ancient and dark. And back to smooth and green again. Under his feet, roots coiled out of the ground and then vanished.

Keep going! shouted Pathseeker. Ellis kept on, stumbling through a gap between branches, against a silver wall, running along a gravel path, around a corner—

—and into a tornado!

Ellis skidded and almost fell. In front of him was a shape like a twisted, boiling storm. The tornado hissed and roared. The air screamed at him. And in the center was the girl, holding the pendant in both hands and staring upward.

This is a vortex! roared Pathseeker in his mind. *A reality storm!*

"Stop!" shouted Ellis.

The girl turned. Her hood had fallen back, and her face had an expression of terror.

"Stay there!" she shouted.

"Stop this!" he shouted again.

"I can't!" she wailed. "It's out of control!"

"What do we do?" Ellis roared.

You have to reach the pendant! said Pathseeker.

Ellis staggered forward, reaching for the Dragon's Eye.

"Help!" the girl shouted. "Oh, no, it's—"

There was a strange sound, almost like a *pop* . . . and the girl disappeared.

The pendant was still there, spinning in the air. The storm was still boiling out of it. Ellis was reaching for the jewel. He tried to pull back, but his momentum carried him on and his hand brushed against it. . . .

Everything seemed to freeze. It was quiet, and the leaves and twigs flying around hung completely still. Looking up, Ellis saw the maze corridors stretching away.

He could see gnarled trees, silver walls, and green hedges. In the distance, he saw himself, staring back in astonishment.

And then the world flipped upside down, and he was gone.

9

LOST

"Ellis? Ellis, wake up!"

Ellis groaned and opened his eyes. Above him was Pathseeker's worried face, looking down. She seemed strange, silver and faint, like a ghost.

"Path?"

Pathseeker smiled, her teeth showing in a wide grin. Ellis sat up.

"What happened?" he asked, rubbing at his

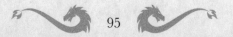

face. He looked around. "Wait . . . where are we?"

"I don't know."

The forest was gone. The silver walls and green hedges had disappeared. Instead ancient stone walls loomed up on either side, worn smooth by time. Above, the sky was no longer blue. It was a deep midnight black. A few stars glinted, but he didn't recognize their patterns.

Ellis stood up. He was still holding his ball of twine. Lifting it, he saw the end of it, snipped off.

"Did I fall asleep?" he asked.

"Ellis, I don't think we're in your world," said Pathseeker. "It feels . . . *different*."

Ellis looked at his dragon. She was still pale.

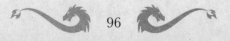

Looking at his hands, he realized that he was the same. And how could Pathseeker be here, anyway? He hadn't summoned her.

"I think we're in a world *between* worlds," said Pathseeker. "Between yours and mine."

"It looks like a maze," said Ellis. "A . . . maze world?"

"I don't know," said the dragon. She sounded worried. "What do we do, Ellis?"

Ellis looked around. Strange stars. Strange walls. "Let's try to find out where we are," he said. He patted Pathseeker's side. "Maybe it will make sense then."

Pathseeker nodded doubtfully.

They
tried flying
first. Ellis sat
on Pathseeker's
back, and she unfurled
her strong wings and lifted.
Pathseeker wasn't a great flier,
but the walls weren't *too* tall, perhaps
twenty feet.

"If we can see the maze, we can map it out," said Ellis. "Get some idea of where we are."

But as Pathseeker rose, beating her wings hard, something strange happened. The walls seemed to grow taller the higher they climbed.

No matter how high they flew, the top was always just out of reach. Looking down, Ellis saw that the ground seemed to have risen as well. After flying as hard as she could, Pathseeker was still a few feet away from the top of the walls and the same distance above the ground.

At last they stopped. Pathseeker settled down again, panting.

"I guess we'll have to solve it from the inside," said Ellis.

But that was strange too. At the first junction, Ellis picked left, and then left again, just as he had for the Green Maze. But the corridors curled and switched, and after a few minutes they ended up at a junction that Ellis was sure he'd seen before. He frowned and scratched an X on one of the stone walls.

"Let's try that again."

He turned left and walked along the path for a few yards to the next junction. He stopped and stared. Scratched on the wall was his X. Ellis looked back—he could almost see where they'd set off! How could this be the same place? He walked back along the path, but when he reached where he was sure they'd started, there was no X.

"Ellis, what's happening?" asked Pathseeker.

Slowly, Ellis took his map and scored out the corridor he'd marked. He started to feel something in the pit of his stomach, a feeling he'd never had before. He *always* knew where he was. He could *always* find his way. But this maze . . .

He scratched another X, wider and deeper, then ran back down the corridor to the next junction. And there it was!

"I don't like this maze," growled Pathseeker. She sniffed at the air. "It *smells* wrong."

Ellis nodded, and then gave a start. Something had flickered past, down one of the corridors.

"Hey!" he shouted. "Hello?"

He ran after it, Pathseeker behind.

"Ellis, be careful!"

He saw the flicker again, and turned left, then right. "Hey!" he roared. "Stop!"

The path branched into three, and he picked a route randomly. "Come back!" he roared. He thought he heard footsteps, and then—

"Argh!"

They crashed into each other. It was the girl in gray! She scrambled to her feet.

"Wait!" called Ellis desperately. She ignored him and raced off the way he'd come. But as she reached the corner, Pathseeker came around it.

The girl gave a cry of shock and fell back. She whipped a knife from her boot and waved it defiantly at the dragon. Her hood had fallen

down, and beneath it her brown hair had
been tied up into a knot. She looked scared
but fierce, and faintly familiar.

"Stay back!" she shouted. She swung the
knife at Pathseeker, who stopped in surprise.
"Back!"

"Stop!" yelled Ellis. "It's okay, she's not dangerous. She's with me!"

The girl stared at Ellis for a moment, and then back at Pathseeker, who gave a friendly, toothy smile.

"I was in the maze, remember?" said Ellis. "I'm Ellis. This is Pathseeker. It's okay, she won't hurt you! She's friendly."

He smiled in what he hoped was a reassuring way. "It's okay," he said again. "You don't have to be scared. What's your name?"

The girl kept her eyes on Pathseeker, and her knife in her hand. She seemed to hesitate. Then she whirled, leapt at Ellis, and held the knife at his throat.

"I," she hissed, "am Princess Skye, daughter

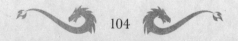

of King Godfic, Royal of the Realm of Draconis, and third in line to the royal throne."

She leaned in close to Ellis. "And if this is your doing, I assure you: my father the king will have your *head*."

10
THE
MAZE REALM

Princess Skye glared at Ellis. "Tell your creature to stay back!" she snarled.

"Um." Ellis could feel the blade of the knife against his throat. He swallowed. "She's not really my creature. I mean, she's my dragon, I suppose, but really I'm her human. I mean, I could *ask* her to stay back?"

"Release him *now*," growled Pathseeker. Ellis had never heard her sound so angry.

But the princess didn't move. Her jaw clenched. "Tell me what you did," she demanded. "Where are we? What is this place? How did we get here?"

"Um," said Ellis again. "Well, Path thinks it's like a world between worlds. But it wasn't us! It was . . . you know . . ." He gulped. "We think it was *you*. With that pendant. . . ."

The girl's eyes blazed, and Ellis closed his eyes. . . . But nothing happened. After a moment he opened them again. She seemed to be thinking.

"Um—" tried Ellis.

"Gaaaaah!" she screamed suddenly. She brought the knife away from Ellis's throat

and threw it so hard into the ground that it embedded itself in the dirt. "How could I be so misled? Awful rotten nasty lying eye!"

Ellis and Pathseeker looked at each other. Pathseeker's shoulders lifted in a shrug.

"Are you okay?" asked Ellis tentatively.

"GAAAAAAH!" shouted the princess again. Then she leaned against the wall and slid down, wrapped her arms around her head, and began to sob.

Ellis stared at her helplessly. "Um . . . there, there," he tried.

"I've *ruined* it!" sobbed the princess. She glared up at Ellis, her face wet with tears. "I was so *close*! I was going to *win*, and then I was going to get the *prize*, and, and—"

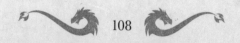

Ellis frowned. "But the prize isn't very big," he said. "I mean, it's just a cup, really. It's—"

"It wasn't about the cup!" she howled.

"Um . . ."

She gave a huge sniff and angrily scrubbed her face with her sleeve. "I was going to go up to Father and say, *Look*, and show him that I could *win* something, and that it wasn't always about my arrogant *brother*!"

"Ohhhh . . ." Ellis nodded. "You mean Prince Harald?"

"Yes!"

"Is he arrogant?" asked Ellis, confused. "Everyone says he's quite clever. He won the—"

"Be quiet!"

"But—"

"Perhaps," said Pathseeker gently, "you should stop trying to help now, Ellis."

Ellis fell silent and stood awkwardly, looking away.

"Princess Skye," said Pathseeker, still in her gentle voice. "I think I understand. You wanted to win the competition to prove to your father that you could, is that right?"

Princess Skye didn't answer, but Pathseeker nodded. "And the Dragon's Eye was going to help you win."

The girl lifted her head. "I heard them talking about it," she said in a dull voice. "Father and his advisors. They said it was magical. That it could find *anything*, if you could get it to

work. Father wanted to find some people. He thought . . ." She gazed at Pathseeker. "He thought there were dragons in Rivven."

Ellis and Pathseeker exchanged worried looks. Princess Skye sniffed.

"They couldn't get it to work. But I looked at it, and it . . . it *looked at me*. And I—I just *knew* I could make it work. But Father wouldn't even

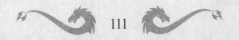

let me try." She scowled. "He never lets me do *anything.*"

"So you . . . borrowed it?" asked Pathseeker. "To win the maze competition?"

The princess nodded. "I thought I'd *show* him, and then he'd trust me, and I could help him find whatever he wanted, you see?"

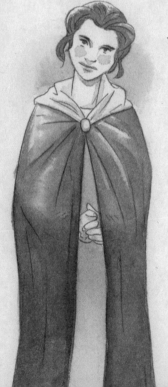

She sighed. "But it all went wrong. I talked to it, and it showed me the right way, but then things *changed.* I could see all the mazes, all at once. I could see the mazes we hadn't even *done* yet."

Ellis thought back to the strangeness in the first maze, looking up and seeing himself in the third maze. And then in the third maze, looking back. He shook his head.

"It's wild dragon magic," said Pathseeker. "From a dark time. It created a reality vortex, like a storm—and when we touched it, the storm brought us here." She sighed. "Wild dragon magic is very dangerous. But you couldn't have known that."

Princess Skye nodded. She'd stopped crying, at least. Her face was red and puffy. But she stood anyway and straightened up. She swallowed, and some of the defiance returned to her.

"So what do we do now?" she asked.

"Well, we're in a maze," said Ellis. "I suppose we just have to solve it."

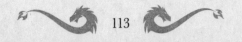

11
ESCAPE

"How do we solve the maze?" asked Princess Skye. "I've been trying already. It's *weird*."

Ellis nodded. "Hmm . . ." He took his ball of twine and wound one end around Princess Skye's knife, still stuck in the dirt. "Let's try this."

The three of them moved off, trailing the twine behind them. They turned left at the first junction, and then right. The paths curled

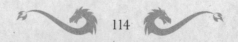

around. Pathseeker called out their directions as they walked, although she seemed a little uncertain.

Princess Skye watched the dragon with an expression that veered between disbelief, fear, and fascination.

"So she's not from our world?" Princess Skye asked.

"No," said Ellis. "And you can ask her yourself, you know."

Pathseeker turned and grinned at her. "I won't bite," she said cheerfully.

Princess Skye gave a rather nervous smile. "You don't . . . eat people?"

"Oh, no," laughed the dragon. "Their clothes would get stuck in my teeth."

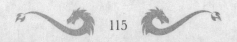

Princess Skye gasped, and Ellis snorted. "Path, don't be mean. No, Your Highness, she doesn't eat people."

"I thought . . . I mean, everyone knows dragons are . . . were . . ."

Pathseeker gave a kinder smile. "Your Highness, the truths that everyone knows are not always very true." She stretched. "And in answer to your other question, no, I'm not from your world. My world is very different."

"Oh," she said. "And do you like our world?"

Pathseeker beamed. "Very much! It is full of interesting things to explore. And I like the humans."

"Oh, no," said Ellis suddenly.

Up ahead of them, at the far end of the path,

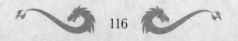

was the knife, still stuck in the dirt. Princess Skye frowned.

"That makes no sense," she said. "We went left, then right. We *can't* be back here."

Pathseeker said, "Perhaps parts of the maze are moving? Like the Silver Maze?"

Ellis shook his head. "I didn't feel anything. And you've been telling me the directions. It doesn't make sense."

"Well," said Princess Skye. "We'll have to try a different route."

They tried again and again. They went right instead of left, then left instead of right. Ellis

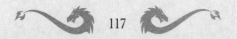

marked every route as they walked down it. They tried scratching marks into the walls, but the marks disappeared, or sometimes seemed to *move*. They argued over the maps Ellis was making, but they knew there was something magical going on. The paths of this maze went over, under, and *through* themselves. They curved in directions that couldn't be drawn.

"Gaaah!" shouted the princess after they ended up back at the knife for the eighth time.

Ellis hung his head. The feeling in his stomach was worse. The thought of being actually lost, unable to simply trace a line from here to there, was terrible.

"It's all *twisted*," he muttered.

Pathseeker had been quiet for some time, plodding along behind them with a distracted look on her broad, bony face. Now she said, "I think we should try something different."

She looked at Princess Skye. "You used the Dragon's Eye," she said. "How?"

The princess frowned. "I just . . . I don't know, really. I thought about what I wanted— a route through the maze."

"Hmm." Pathseeker nodded. "We're lost between worlds, Ellis. When you bring me to your world, what do you do?"

"Drun says it's like making a space in your heart," said Ellis. "For the connection."

"Perhaps we need to make our own

connection," said Pathseeker. "Back to the maze where we were."

"But *how*?" asked the princess.

Ellis stared at his maps, drawn and redrawn. They weren't like his beautiful, neat maps at home, so careful and correct. This was *chaos*. His pencil was almost worn away.

He gazed up at the stars. Could he use those to navigate? But somehow he knew they would move too.

"Look up," murmured Pathseeker.

Ellis frowned. "That's what Tom said."

Pathseeker nodded. "Not just that," she said. "He said . . ." Her face creased as she thought about it. "He said we have to *experience* things."

Ellis stared at her, baffled. "I don't understand."

Pathseeker shook her head. "I didn't either. But I think he meant *make a connection*. This realm isn't normal—it's magic. You have to make a connection to where we left, something . . ."

Ellis flicked back through his notes, to the map of the Dark Maze. There it was, clear and precise, each curve and twist, despite the maze's being so complicated. Even parts where the paths had gone over or under were all neatly laid out. He stared at it.

Make a connection, he thought, but nothing happened. Frowning, he tried to focus on the

point where he'd found Princess Skye. On the entrance. On anywhere.

Nothing happened.

It was just marks on paper. It was pleasing

and neat, but there was nothing to hold on to. Nothing like the sight, or sound, or scent . . .

Scent . . .

Just for a moment, he remembered the faint scent of lime.

"Do you remember a smell of limes?" he asked slowly. The others stared at him.

"Yes," said Princess Skye suddenly. "In the Dark Maze. It was a lime tree in a clearing."

"Yes, that's right!" said Ellis. "There was a lime tree. We came around the corner, and it was suddenly very sunny. There was a break in the trees, and there was this lime tree. . . ."

"Covered in tiny white flowers," said the princess.

Ellis nodded. He tried to remember it as closely as possible. It seemed important. "It was moving slightly. There was a breeze. And two exits, one northwest, one east by—"

"No," interrupted Pathseeker. She gazed into Ellis's face. "Think about the *tree*."

Ellis tried to hold it in his head. He'd been so busy with his map, but the forest maze had been all around him. The smell of damp earth and green moss. The sound of tiny leaves shivering in the breeze and the swaying of branches. The feel of bark under his hands as he crawled. The silvery light from cobwebs stuck between twigs, and the hum of bees . . . All these things. They were *real*.

"Something's happening!"

Ellis looked up. Princess Skye was staring down the path at a bright, shining point. It was the size of a doorway and seemed to swirl. In this world of dark stone, it glowed.

"What is it?" asked Princess Skye.

"I think it's the way back," murmured Pathseeker. "Oh, well done, Ellis!"

Ellis stepped up to it carefully. The walls of the maze seemed to grow higher and darker as if the maze was *angry*. He reached out one hand, almost touching the swirling space. With his other hand, he reached behind him for Pathseeker and grasped her rough shoulder.

"Your Highness," he said. "Hold on to Pathseeker."

Princess Skye looked at the dragon nervously,

and then reached out a hand and touched her

shoulder.

"Are you sure?" she asked. She sounded scared, but she stood next to Ellis bravely.

"I think so!" said Ellis.

Still, he hesitated. This made no sense— not *map* sense. There was nothing behind the swirling light. It wasn't *logical*.

And then he felt the air move slightly. A breeze came from out of the shape, and a scent of lime.

Ellis closed his eyes and stepped forward.

12
PATHSEEKER

There was light all around them. Ellis could tell that much, even with his eyes closed. The light was so white and sharp that it seemed to go right through them. Ellis had a strange feeling of *folding*, or unfolding, and then . . .

. . . and then he crashed to the ground, and felt tree roots and soil under his hands. He turned and looked up to see Pathseeker

hurtling through the air, and then Princess Skye landed next to him with a grunt.

Ellis looked around. They were in the small clearing, filled with pale sunlight and the scent of the lime tree and its tiny white flowers.

"We made it!" he shouted. "We're back in our world!"

Princess Skye grinned, but Pathseeker sniffed and looked around. "Something's still wrong," she hissed. Ellis realized he could feel it too. There was a pulsing, shaking feeling, coming from up ahead. The woody maze was shifting in color, from green to silver. . . .

"The vortex is still going!" he shouted.

Ellis ran forward to the center of the maze and staggered to a stop. There was the Dragon's

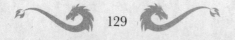

Eye pendant, hanging in the air. Above the pendant was the swirling storm of changing walls and colors. Inside the pendant, the single angry eye glared at them in fury.

"It's even worse!" shouted the princess. "What do we do?"

"I don't know!" Ellis called back.

As they watched, the Dragon's Eye drifted toward them. The walls of the maze flickered green and silver. The air swirled like a tornado, howling and vicious.

"That's *quite* enough of that," said Pathseeker suddenly. She stepped forward and snatched the stone clean out of the air using her mouth. The pendant screamed, but she chomped once, twice, swallowed . . .

. . . and the storm stopped.

Ellis stared at Pathseeker with his mouth open. She smiled back.

"Dragon magic can't hurt *me*," she said cheerfully. "I *am* dragon magic!"

"Wow!" Ellis slung his arms around Pathseeker and hugged her rough green hide. "That was amazing!"

Pathseeker purred with pleasure. "Now," she said. "Time to leave this place, I think."

Princess Skye said, "That might be a problem."

Ellis turned and saw what she meant.

The Dragon's Eye was gone, but the chaos it had created was still there. The maze was bizarre now—a mix of ancient woods, neat green hedges, moving silver walls, and dark, ancient stone. It stretched in all directions and upward as well, winding over and under and around and through itself in ways that Ellis couldn't even follow. It seemed to stretch on for miles and miles.

"Ah . . . ," sighed Pathseeker.

Ellis looked at her. She was curling in on herself, and her eyes were closed. The ridges on her back trembled.

"What's wrong with her?" asked Princess Skye.

"I don't know," said Ellis. "Maybe it was the pendant—maybe it *can* hurt her!"

But Pathseeker waved a paw. "No," she growled. "I think . . . Ellis, I think I'm getting my power!"

Ellis gasped as he understood. "It's okay," he said excitedly to Princess Skye. "This is what happens to dragons. They have a special power, each one different. Pathseeker's getting hers!"

Pathseeker seemed to grow. She stood tall, and her green skin rippled, and she laughed.

"Ah . . . ," she said. "I can see! I can see the way out! Follow me!"

She turned abruptly and trotted off. Then,

to the children's astonishment, the dragon walked straight into a silver wall—and through it!

"What—" started Ellis.

"Where did she go?" asked Princess Skye.

Pathseeker's head poked back through the wall. "Come on!"

Ellis reached forward and tried to touch the wall, but his hand passed right through.

"It's not real," he murmured.

"It's an illusion," said Pathseeker, grinning. "But I can see, Ellis. That's my power—I can see through illusions. I can see what's *real*! Come on!"

She disappeared again. Ellis reached for Princess Skye's hand and stepped through the

silver wall, and they found themselves in a long, woody corridor.

"This way!" chuckled Pathseeker.

She scurried through the maze, taking left and right turns through walls, ignoring everything Ellis and the princess could see. Gradually Ellis started to recognize the route.

He remembered that the next turn was a left, then right after a hundred yards. Pulling his map from his bag, he checked and grinned.

"This is the way we came in," he said. "It looks all wrong, but Path can see what's really there. We're nearly out!"

As he said it, he realized that the illusion was fading. Now the maze was mostly trees and thick, gnarly branches. The ground was roots, and the junctions and openings were real. Suddenly they were at the entrance, and they could hear shouts from outside.

"Well," said Pathseeker. "Time for me to disappear."

Ellis smiled. "See you soon, Path. Oh, we'll be able to tell everyone about your new power!"

Pathseeker grinned, and then turned to the princess. "Your Highness," she said, bowing her head.

Princess Skye bowed back. "Thank you," she said. "I promise I won't tell anyone about you."

Then Pathseeker started to fade, fainter and fainter, until she was just a ghost. . . .

Then she was gone.

"Ready?" asked Ellis.

The princess pulled her hood up and nodded. "Ready."

They left the maze.

13
LOOKING UP

"It's them!" shouted a voice as Ellis and Princess Skye stepped out of the maze. "They're out!"

The area in front of them was full of people milling around. They looked worried, then relieved when they saw the children.

"Oh, thank *goodness*," said the nice lady from the flag table. "We thought you were terribly lost!"

She held up their two balls of twine, one

green, one gray. "Why in the world would you cut your strings?" she asked, looking a little cross. "We were trying to find you!"

There was a ragged cheer from the crowd, which was smaller than before. Ellis noticed that it was getting dark. They'd been in the maze for hours.

"Sorry," he said. "I, ah . . . I got tangled. . . ."

"*I* got tangled," said Princess Skye. "And this boy helped me." She pulled back her hood, and the lady gasped.

"Your Highness!" She curtsied. "I'm sorry. I didn't—"

"It's fine," said the princess curtly. "See me back to the palace, please. Is my father still here?"

"No, Your Highness. He and the prince left some time ago."

"Good. Then there's no reason to bother them, is there?"

The woman looked worried. "The king asked where you were," she said. "When you didn't join them onstage."

"It's been a long day," said Princess Skye firmly. "I'm sure the king is tired. I'll tell him in the morning. Now, please help me home."

She pulled her hood up again, and they walked off. She said nothing to Ellis and seemed to have forgotten he even existed.

Well, that was a bit rude, whispered Pathseeker's voice. Ellis shrugged.

But just as she turned to leave the gardens, the princess looked back. For a moment, she gazed at Ellis with a thoughtful expression. Then she gave a tiny nod. Ellis smiled and nodded back.

"Hey, slowfeet!"

Ellis turned. Cara and the others were

walking up to him. Cara was holding a small silver trophy.

"Hey," he said. "So you won?"

Cara grinned. "Just ahead of Connor. Prince Harald shook my hand. He's *very* handsome, you know. So what happened to you? And where's the other girl?"

Ellis shook his head. "Let's get home," he said. "And then I have a story for you."

Two days later, Ellis sat with the others on the pier. He dangled his feet over the water and ate fried cod scraps. It was sunny, but there was still a fresh spring breeze off the water. Ellis felt the breeze and listened to the sound of water lapping. He watched the ships dock.

"What did Chancellor Berin say?" asked Tom.

"She was pleased, I think." Ellis frowned. "I thought she might be cross that the Dragon's Eye was . . . um, broken." It seemed strange to say "eaten." "But she seemed relieved. I think she was worried the king might use it to find the Guild Hall." He smiled. "She was very pleased with Path. She said her new power would be very useful. To be able to see through illusions, to see what really mattered." Berin had bowed to Pathseeker, and told them both "Well done," and Pathseeker had blushed with pride and happiness. Thinking about it, Ellis smiled again.

Cara grinned. "I bet old Godfic was spitting when he found out the Eye was gone."

"And it really was the princess?" asked Mira. "I mean, *really*?"

"Yeah."

"Wow. Friends in high places, eh?"

Ellis grinned.

"It's strange, though," Connor said. "She used the Eye. You're only supposed to be able to do that if you're a dragonseer. Do you think she *is*?"

"What about that dragon I saw at the palace, the night of the fire?" Tom asked. "Do you think that might have been hers?"

"I don't know." Ellis thought about it. "She was pretty surprised to see Pathseeker. But . . . not as scared as you'd think. You know, it did seem like she'd seen a dragon before. It's a mystery."

He shrugged and stood up. "Come on. We've got to head back for afternoon classes."

"We've got ages yet," said Cara lazily.

"I know." Ellis waved his map. "But I want to go up Haywain Road. There are some little side streets there I haven't mapped yet."

The others groaned. But they all got up and headed back anyway.

"Still obsessed, then, eh?" laughed Tom as they walked.

Ellis smiled. "Maybe. But you were right

about experiencing things. If it hadn't been for you, we would never have escaped the Maze Realm. Maybe I'll try to look up a bit more."

Ellis made a show of looking up, and found he was staring right at the palace, on top of the huge rock at the center of Rivven. He scanned

the tiny windows. Was Princess Skye looking out just now? Would she be able to see them from all the way up there?

And then he heard that wonderful whisper in his head, the one that had been his constant friend ever since that campfire a year ago— the whisper that reminded him that his life was more extraordinary than he could ever have imagined.

Look up, whispered Pathseeker, amused. *See what's really there. . . .*

Ellis frowned and looked again at the palace. He looked at the huge rock. The huge, high rock, right at the heart of Rivven, bigger than the palace itself, big enough to hold . . .

"Oh!" he said suddenly, and laughed.

"What's up?" asked Cara.

Ellis shook his head. "Nothing," he said. "I'd been trying to work out where something was, and Pathseeker just helped me figure it out." He grinned. "Come on. Let's head back. I've got some maps to update."

They made their way back to the tiny entrance in the old cottage that would lead them through winding, turning corridors to the Dragonseer Guild Hall, hidden in the heart of the city.

THE DRAGON STORM IS COMING.

Soar into adventure with dragonseer
Mira and her dragon, Flameteller!

The banner had a picture of a horrible, fierce dragon, breathing fire. Next to the dragon was a man wearing a crown and armor, holding a long spear. He was stabbing the dragon, and the dragon was writhing in agony.

DEATH TO DRAGGUNS, read the sign.

Is that supposed to be us? asked Flameteller's voice. Mira nodded.

There was a buzz of activity around them. Posters had been pinned up all around, and

Mira heard shouting up ahead. Berin's face was grim.

"Stay close to me, students," she said. "And remember: if anyone asks, you are apprentice clerks."

They walked toward the King's Plaza, an open square that was sometimes a marketplace, sometimes a festival area. Today there was a stage with red-and-gold drapes. A crowd was gathering. To the side sat a black carriage with four beautiful black horses. The carriage had no crest or other markings, and its curtains were closed.

A herald stepped onto the stage.

"My good people of Rivven!" he called in a barrel-chested roar.

The crowd stopped chattering and turned. The herald held up a scroll. "I bring a proclamation from His Majesty, King Godfic! He instructs me on this day to tell you—"

"I'll handle this," called a voice, and the herald stopped in surprise. Mira realized the carriage door had opened and a hooded figure now stood next to it. The figure leaped lightly onto the stage, patted the startled man on the back, and lifted his hood.

It was Prince Harald, the king's son! He handed his hooded cloak to his personal attendant. The crowd gasped, and many of them knelt, but he waved them back to their feet.

"No, no," he said. "Thank you, but I am not your king. Please, stand."

Prince Harald was rather handsome, Mira thought. He had shoulder-length blond hair and a friendly face. He wore a red outfit decorated with silver thread patterns. He smiled as the people stood again.

"As you know," he said, "my father counts the safety of Rivven and the land of Draconis above all things. He protects us from evil. But there are rumors of a danger from our past, come to haunt us again."

His voice was serious, and as he looked around, the people stayed hushed.

"I am talking about dragons," he said.

Mira gasped. Beside her, Berin pursed her lips but showed no other expression.

"We had not wanted to believe it," said the prince. "But recently an item under royal protection was stolen from the king's own chambers. It was a tool of old magic. Old *dragon magic*. And it can only be used by those who are in league with dragons."

There was a burst of excited chatter, but Prince Harald spoke over it.

"There are those who have chosen to side with dragons, against their own kind!" he roared. "They pretend to be your friends, but secretly they bring back these terrible creatures! They are here in Rivven—perhaps in this very square!"

Everyone in the crowd looked around, peering into each other's faces, searching for guilt. Berin's face stayed calm, and she gazed at the prince as if mildly interested in a curious idea. Mira and the others tried to copy her. The city, normally so friendly and bustling, suddenly felt very hostile.

"My father, King Godfic, Dragon Scourge,

is sworn to protect Draconis," continued Prince Harald. "And he has ordered me to root out these traitors! We will search every building in this city, and we will not stop until we have found them *and* their terrible creatures . . . and *destroyed* them! Who's with me?"

The crowd *roared* with a mix of anger and delight. They cheered and thumped each other on the backs.

Berin sighed. "This is no place for children," she said primly. "Come along."

She led them away from the square.

"That's all *lies*!" snapped Erin. "Why would he say that?"

"Quiet now," murmured Berin. "We'll discuss it later."